For Alfie James Yarrow, born June 27, 2008.
With love, C.M. xxx

First American edition published in 2009 by Boxer Books Limited.

Distributed in the United States and Canada by
Sterling Publishing Co., Inc. 387 Park Avenue South, New York, NY 10016-8810

First published in Great Britain in 2009 by Boxer Books Limited.
www.boxerbooks.com

Text and illustrations copyright © 2009 Cathy MacLennan
Spooky Doo font copyright © 2009 Cathy MacLennan

The illustrations were prepared using acrylic paints on blue kraft paper.
The text is set in Spooky Doo.

ISBN 978-1-906250-67-6
1 3 5 7 9 10 8 6 4 2
Printed in China

All of our papers are sourced from managed forests and renewable resources.

Spooky Spooky Spooky!

Cathy MacLennan

Boxer Books

Velvety,
velvety
bats . . .

And horrible howling cats.

Webby
webs

and spider

eggs . . .

Then lots and lots and lots of legs.

Spooky spooky spooky!

Rotten rats and bug-eyed flies,
gobbling up the pumpkin pies.

Spooky spooky spooky!

Meander, meander,
slip slimy snails,

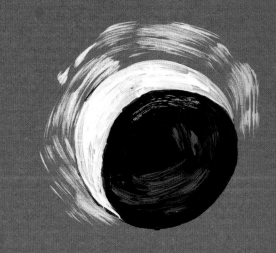

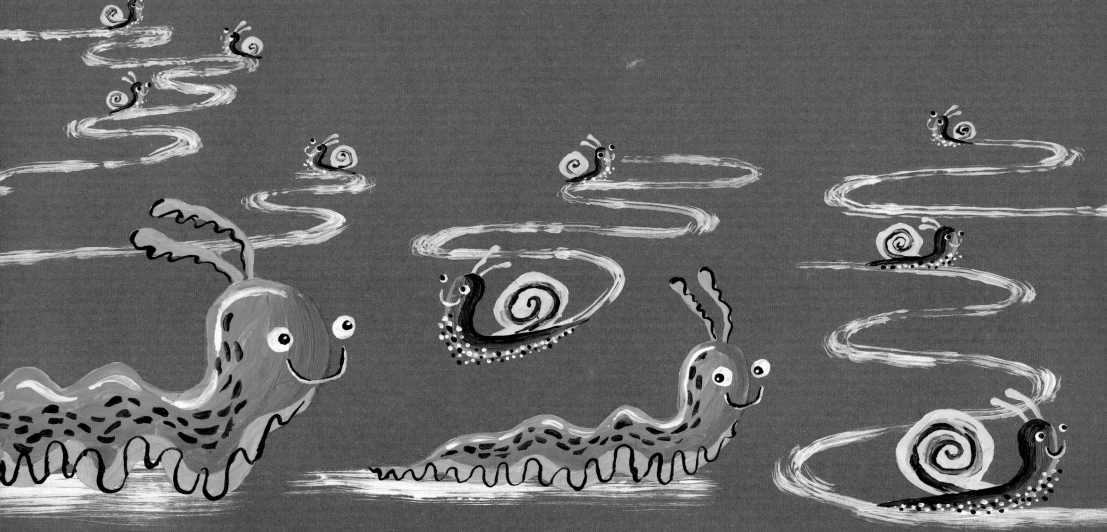

slithery slugs and silver trails.
Spooky spooky spooky!

Plants that climb
and plants that curl,
Wings that swoosh
and eyes that swirl.

Spooky spooky spooky!

The moon, the moon!
What's happened
to the moon?
It's dark,
it's dark,
it's very,
very dark!

On come the lights

Then bright toothy smiles

and light-up eyes.

Out come the
trick-or-treaters to play!

AWAY go
bats and cats,
spiders and rats,
owls and bugs,
snails and slugs.

HOORAY HOORAY
HOORAY!